BENNY'S VISIT

BENNY'S VISIT

For my friend, Gill
L.M.J.

Text copyright © Linda M. Jennings 1988
Illustrations copyright © Krystyna Turska 1988

First published 1988 by Hodder and Stoughton Children's Books

Picturemac edition published 1991 by
MACMILLAN CHILDREN'S BOOKS
A division of Pan Macmillan Children's Books Limited
London and Basingstoke
Associated companies throughout the world

Reprinted 1991

ISBN 0-333-49966-2

A CIP catalogue record for this book is available from
the British Library

Printed in Hong Kong

BENNY'S VISIT

LINDA M. JENNINGS

Illustrated by KRYSTYNA TURSKA

MACMILLAN CHILDREN'S BOOKS

Once, a very long time ago, there was a dog called Benny who lived with an old tramp.

Their home was a broken-down barge moored in the backwater of a canal. The roof of the barge leaked, and the painted flowers had long since faded. But Tom the tramp would block up the holes with old newspapers so it was cosy enough, and it was, in any case, the only home the two of them knew.

Sometimes, when the sun was hot, Benny would lie stretched out on the cabin roof, keeping one eye open, so that he could see what was going on up and down the canal. Tom didn't bother. He liked to keep himself to himself, and besides, people could be very funny sometimes about an old tramp with holes in his boots and a long, straggly yellow beard.

Benny often wondered what it would be like to live with a family in a proper house. Would the children romp and play with him? Would they feed him with sticky sweets and pieces of cake as they sometimes did when no one was watching? Perhaps he would have a mutton pie for every meal instead of only once a week, which was all old Tom could afford.

More than anything else Benny liked to watch the children playing on the towpath. He longed to play with them, but when he tried mothers and nursemaids would pull their young charges to them, crying:

"Keep away from that dirty old dog – he's probably got fleas."

Benny would feel very hurt then. Of course he hadn't got fleas. Not when he swam in the canal every single day.

Now, one sunny summer's day Benny was lying in his usual position on the cabin roof, his head nodding and his wakeful eye closing, despite itself. Suddenly, *splash!* something landed near him in the water.

It was a red shiny ball.

"Mama," wailed a little boy. "I've lost my ball. It's over there, by that old barge."

Benny saw his chance to introduce
himself at last to a family of children.
In a flash, he was up and into the water.
  "Look, Mama, that dog's found my ball.
Look, Mama, he's bringing it back to me!"

"He looks *dreadfully* dirty," said Mama,
as Benny scrambled up the bank,
shook himself, and dropped the ball
at the little boy's feet.

Now Benny had led a rough and tough sort of life. He was a bit scruffy, but he had a friendly air about him, and big, affectionate brown eyes. Old Tom had taught him to sit up and shake a paw, and the little boy and his sister were enchanted.

"Mama, he's so clever," said Henry.

"Mama, can we take him home with us?" pleaded Charlotte. "*Please.*"

"Of *course* not," said Mama. "We couldn't have a dog like that in the house. The very idea."

But Charlotte had a piece of gingerbread in her hand and, as the little family made its way homeward, she broke the gingerbread into small pieces and scattered it along the ground.

Benny followed eagerly. It was the first thing he had eaten all day. And perhaps, at last, he would discover what it would be like to visit a real family.

"Oh, how annoying," said Mama, flapping her parasol at poor Benny. "That dog has come home with us. Go away, dog, shoo!"

"He knows we want him to live with us," said Charlotte. She hung on to her mother's arm, and smiled up at her. "He's such a *clever* dog, Mama. And he would be quite handsome once he's had a bath."

Mama gave a big sigh. "Oh, very well," she said. "But he's your dog, and you must look after him. He's to live in the scullery, and he must have a bath *at once*."

Benny didn't enjoy his bath very much. He didn't like the soap in his eyes, and he didn't like his nice doggy smell disappearing in a steamy cloud of scented air. Charlotte dusted him with violet-scented powder, and Henry tied his hair with a blue ribbon.

I look stupid, thought Benny, as he padded downstairs behind them towards his new home in the scullery.

The scullery was dark, with a stone
floor and a tiny, dirty window.
A green light came into the room from
the ivy pressing against the glass.
Henry put down a bowl of water and
some scraps.

"We will have to go to tea now,"
said Charlotte. "But we'll be back
later." She pressed her mouth against
Benny's furry ear. "Perhaps I can steal
you some of *my* tea," she whispered.

When they had gone Benny pushed his
nose round the scraps of bread and
bacon fat. I hope she won't forget,
he thought sadly.

Charlotte brought back some rather
sticky cherry pie and a chocolate biscuit.
Then Henry took a long rope, and tied it
round Benny's neck.

"Mama says you must have a lead," he
said. "But this will have to do
for the moment."

Then the two children and Benny were out in the sunlight, and Benny saw an enormous green lawn and flower-beds and a huge spreading cedar tree. He pulled at his rope, and nearly choked.

"Heel, sir," said Henry sternly.

Poor Benny! He longed to race over the velvet lawn and splash into the fishpond. He had never had anything around his neck in his life, and he didn't like the feeling. With one enormous tug he had pulled the rope from Henry's hand. He was free!

"Come here, sir," shouted Henry. "*Heel!*"

Benny took no notice. He ran and he ran, right across the lawn and over the flower-bed.

It so happened that the children's mother had invited all the members of the Church Ladies' Sewing Circle to play a game of croquet and enjoy afternoon tea on the lawn. Croquet was a game where you hit a wooden ball through a little hoop, and Benny thought it looked great fun. Before the children could catch him he had rushed joyfully across the grass and joined in.

Suddenly Benny caught sight of a group of ladies sitting at a little table in the sunshine, enjoying a plateful of cucumber sandwiches, a cream sponge-cake and some iced buns.

There was one thing that old Tom had never taught Benny and that was that you didn't steal cakes from ladies sitting in the sunshine enjoying their afternoon tea – and the cakes did look very good indeed!

Benny was in disgrace. He had trampled all over Mama's flower-beds and broken down her carnations. He had ruined the Church Ladies' tea party. Now he sat in the yard, tethered by a rope to a post. Somewhere he could smell the most delicious meal cooking.

Quickly, Benny began to gnaw at his rope.

Now, as you know, Benny was a rough and tough kind of dog. Indeed he had a criminal record, for many was the meal he had stolen from the butcher's shop. So when he had finally bitten through the rope, and noticed that the kitchen door was ajar he didn't hesitate...

Benny did not see the cook, ladling soup from a large tureen. He did not see the kitchen-maid, straining the vegetables. His eyes were on a wonderful golden roast goose sitting on a platter.

With a bound, Benny was across the kitchen and at the table.

"Take *that!*" yelled the cook, flinging the ladle at poor Benny, just as his jaws clamped around the goose.

"And *that,*" shouted the kitchen-maid, hitting Benny with a saucepan. He let go of the goose and put his tail between his legs.

Benny raced out of the door just in time to avoid the saucepan full of hot water that followed him.

Benny lay panting in the shrubbery behind the lawn. He heard Charlotte and Henry calling him.

"Bruno," shouted Henry. "Come here, Bruno." Bruno was his new name. Benny didn't like it very much. "Bruno, Bruno, suppertime!"

Benny was hungry, sore and cold. The bath had made his coat all light and fluffy, and the wind blew through it. He was almost tempted to go back to the children, who loved him, even if Mama didn't, but instead he shook off his blue ribbon.

When the voices finally faded he rolled in a nice smelly patch under the tree. He felt more like the old Benny again. It was time to go home.

The sun was setting as Benny trotted back along the canal towpath. Ahead of him he saw old Tom with a bag in his hand. And Benny could smell – mutton pie!

"Come on, old friend, suppertime," said Tom. "We've got company, I see!"